Whispers of Justice

Whispers of Justice

UNRAVELING A WEB OF DECEIT

Anurag Anurag

Anurag Anurag

Contents

1   A Town Shattered ... 1

2   Unraveling the Web ... 4

3   The Unseen Shadows ... 7

4   Shadows of Deception ... 11

5   The Web of Motives ... 14

6   The Shady Dealings ... 17

7   The Deep Dive ... 21

8   The Informant's End ... 25

9   Unmasking Deceit: The Night of Revelations ... 29

10   The Prodigal Son's Deception ... 32

11   The Unseen Alibi: Robert Caldwell's Enigma ... 36

12   The Drug Lord's Dilemma: A Trail of Shadows ... 40

13   Unveiling Deception ... 43

14   Veil of Obscurity ... 46

15   The Illusion of Guilt ... 49

16   Closing In ... 52

17   A New Dawn ... 55

1

A Town Shattered

Ravenswood, a town once known for its tranquility and peace, was abruptly awakened from its serene slumber by the tremors of a horrifying revelation. The calm and quiet that once defined the town was shattered by the news of a brutal murder. The victim was none other than James Thornton, a man of wealth and influence, renowned for his lavish life-style and an extensive list of adversaries. His lifeless body was found within the confines of his luxurious mansion, a grim contrast to the grandeur that surrounded it.

The responsibility of leading the investigation fell on the shoulders of Detective Laura Thompson, a figure held in high regard within the ranks of the town's police force. Her reputation as a seasoned detective, known for her sharp instincts and unwavering determination, was well-known throughout the town. Accompanied by her partner, Detective Mike Rodriguez, a trusted comrade in the pursuit of justice, she rushed to the crime scene. As they arrived, the air seemed to thicken with the weight of the town's hidden secrets, their presence growing more ominous.

Stepping into the estate, Laura and Mike were met with a heavy sense of dread. The mansion, once a testament to James Thornton's success, was now a silent witness to the aftermath of a violent act committed by an unknown perpetrator. The opulence of the mansion stood in stark contrast to the grim reality of the crime scene. Laura's experienced eyes scanned the surroundings, searching for the subtle details that could help unravel the mystery.

Ravenswood, a town used to the soft whispers of gossip and intrigue, suddenly found itself in the harsh glare of a mystery that went beyond the ordinary. The town, with its cobbled streets and centuries-old archi-tecture, was now the keeper of a dark secret. A secret that would require the investigative skills of Detective Laura Thompson to uncover and bring to light.

As Laura and Mike delved deeper into the mansion, they could feel the tension in the air. The mansion was eerily quiet, the silence only broken by the occasional creaking of the old wooden floorboards under their feet. The opulent decor and expensive art pieces adorning the walls seemed to mock the grim reality of the situation.

Suddenly, Laura stopped in her tracks. Her sharp eyes had caught a glimpse of something unusual. A faint, almost imperceptible, smudge on the otherwise immaculate marble floor. Bending down, she carefully examined it. It was a shoe print, but not just any shoe print. It was a very specific one, a type only worn by a certain group of people in Ravenswood. This was the first tangible clue they had found, and it sent a shiver down Laura's spine.

Meanwhile, Mike had ventured into the study, a room filled with shelves of books and personal artifacts. His eyes were drawn to a picture frame turned face-down on the desk. As he picked it up, he was met with the smiling faces of James Thornton and another man, their arms around each other. The man was familiar, but he couldn't quite place him. The picture seemed to hold significance, but the question was - what?

The discovery of these clues added a new layer of complexity to the case. The peaceful town of Ravenswood was not as it seemed, and as the investigation progressed, it became clear that the secrets it held were far darker than anyone could have imagined. The whispers of justice grew louder, echoing through the misty streets, as Laura and Mike found themselves tangled in a web of deceit and betrayal.

2

〜

Unraveling the Web

Laura began her day with a visit to the local cobbler, an elderly man named Mr. Jenkins who had been crafting and repairing shoes in Ravenswood for decades. He confirmed Laura's suspicions - the shoe print was indeed unique, belonging to a type of shoe worn by a certain group in Ravenswood. This revelation opened a new line of inquiry for Laura, providing her with a list of potential suspects.

Meanwhile, Mike was engrossed in the town's old records, trying to identify the man in the picture with James Thornton. After hours of research and conversations with long-time residents, he discovered that the man was a former business partner of Thornton's, a man named Robert Caldwell who had supposedly moved away years ago. But why was his picture in Thornton's study? The plot was thickening.

As Laura and Mike delved deeper, they uncovered a web of secrets and lies that ran deep in the town's history. They found out that James Thornton was not just a businessman, but also involved in some shady dealings. The peaceful facade of Ravenswood was starting to crack, revealing a darker side.

Their investigation did not go unnoticed. There were forces in Ravenswood that wanted the secrets to remain buried and would stop at nothing to ensure that. One night, as Laura was going through the list of people who wore the unique shoes, she noticed a shadow outside her window. Before she could react, a brick wrapped in a threatening note crashed through the window. The message was clear - stop digging or face the consequences.

Laura, shaken but undeterred, found another clue at the crime scene that was previously overlooked. It was a small piece of fabric, possibly from the killer's clothing. But just as she was about to examine it, an unknown assailant attacked her.

The following morning, Laura woke up in the hospital with a throbbing headache. The events of the previous night were a blur, but the piece of fabric was still tightly clutched in her hand. Despite the attack, her resolve only strengthened. She knew she was on the right path.

Meanwhile, Mike was growing increasingly worried about Laura. He decided to pay a visit to Robert Caldwell, the man in the picture. Mike planned to go and meet Robert.

Back in Ravenswood, Laura, now discharged from the hospital, decided to pay a visit to the people on her list. One by one, she started questioning them, their reactions varying from shock to fear to outright hostility. But Laura was undeterred. She knew that the key to solving the murder mystery was hidden among these people.

Laura and Mike found themselves at a crossroads. The web of deceit was more tangled than they had anticipated. Every clue they found only led to more questions. But they knew they were close. The truth was within their grasp, and they were determined to uncover it, no matter what the cost.

3

❧

The Unseen Shadows

Laura began her day with a renewed sense of determination. Despite the attack and the looming threat, she was more resolved than ever to solve the murder mystery. She knew that every moment was crucial and that she had to act fast.

Meanwhile, Mike was on his way to meet Robert Caldwell. The drive to the outskirts of Ravenswood was long and filled with anticipation. As he pulled up to Caldwell's modest home, he couldn't help but wonder about the man's connection to the murder.

Back in Ravenswood, Laura was making progress. She had managed to narrow down her list of suspects. Each person she questioned revealed a new piece of the puzzle, bringing her one step closer to solving the mystery. But with each revelation, the danger grew. She knew she was treading on thin ice.

As Mike sat across from Caldwell, he couldn't help but feel a sense of unease. Caldwell was cooperative, answering all of Mike's questions, but there was something about him that didn't sit right with Mike. He decided to dig deeper.

In Ravenswood, Laura's investigation took a sudden turn. One of the suspects, a man named George, revealed a shocking piece of information. He claimed to have seen James Thornton arguing with a mysterious stranger the night before the murder. This was a breakthrough Laura had been waiting for.

Meanwhile, Mike's conversation with Caldwell took a surprising turn. Caldwell confessed to having a falling out with Thornton over a business deal gone wrong. He admitted to harboring resentment towards Thornton but denied having anything to do with his murder.

Laura and Mike found themselves in the eye of the storm. The peaceful town of Ravenswood was turning out to be a labyrinth of secrets and lies. But they were not deterred. They knew they had to face the unseen shadows to bring justice to James Thornton.

Laura received an anonymous tip about a secret meeting that was supposed to take place that night. She knew it was risky, but she decided to go. As she stepped into the shadows, she could feel the danger lurking around. But she was ready. She knew she was on the brink of a major breakthrough.

Armed with the anonymous tip, Laura decided to stake out the location of the secret meeting. She arrived under the cover of darkness, her heart pounding in her chest. The location was an abandoned warehouse on the outskirts of Ravenswood, a place that had seen better days.

Inside the warehouse, Laura could make out the faint outlines of two figures. She strained her ears, trying to catch snippets of their hushed conversation. Suddenly, a familiar name echoed through the silence - George, one of her suspects. This confirmed her suspicion that George was more involved in the case than he had let on.

Meanwhile, Mike was back in Ravenswood, examining the piece of fabric Laura had found at the crime scene. It was a unique pattern, one he had seen before. A sudden realization hit him - it matched the lining of a jacket worn by a member of a local gang known for their unique footwear, the same as the shoe print found at the crime scene.

As Laura continued her surveillance, she noticed something else. One of the figures was limping, a detail that could be crucial in identifying him. She made a mental note of it, promising herself to cross-reference this information with medical records in Ravenswood.

Back in town, Mike decided to pay a visit to the local tailor, hoping to confirm his suspicions about the fabric. The tailor recognized the pattern immediately, confirming Mike's suspicion. It was indeed the lining used in jackets made for the local gang.

Laura and Mike found themselves a step closer to solving the murder mystery. The shoe print, the fabric, the anonymous tip, and now the limp - all pieces of a puzzle that was starting to form a coherent picture. But they knew they were not out of the woods yet. The unseen shadows of Ravenswood still held many secrets, waiting to be uncovered.

4

∽

Shadows of Deception

The town of Ravenswood was still reeling from the shock of the attack on Laura. The tranquility that once defined the town was now replaced by a palpable tension. Laura, however, was not one to be easily deterred.

Laura's first order of business was to revisit the clues they had gathered so far - the shoe print, the fabric, and the information about George. She decided to pay George another visit. His reaction to her questions during their last encounter had raised her suspicions. However, George had a solid alibi for the night of the murder, effectively removing him from her list of suspects. This was a setback, but Laura was not discouraged.

Meanwhile, Mike was following up on the lead about the fabric. His visit to the local tailor had confirmed his suspicions - the fabric was indeed from a jacket worn by a local gang known for their unique foot-wear. This was a significant breakthrough. It not only corroborated the clue about the shoe print but also gave them a new lead to follow.

As Laura and Mike delved deeper into the investigation, they found themselves navigating a web of deceit and betrayal. Every clue they uncovered revealed a new layer of complexity in the case. But they were not deterred. They knew they were close to uncovering the truth.

Back in town, Mike was making progress with the gang angle. He managed to narrow down the members who wore the unique shoes and owned the jacket with the specific fabric. However, all of them had strong alibis for the night of the murder. This was another setback, but Mike was not ready to give up.

Laura had been on high alert since the attack. She knew her assailant was someone local, someone who had a lot to lose if she solved the murder mystery. The distinct tattoo of a raven on his arm was the only clue she had about his identity.

She decided to pay a visit to the local tattoo parlors in Ravenswood, hoping to find the artist who had inked the raven tattoo. After visiting several parlors and showing them a sketch of the tattoo, she finally found the artist. He remembered the tattoo well as it was a unique design requested by a local gang member.

With this information, Laura was able to narrow down her list of suspects. She cross-referenced this with the list of people who wore the unique shoes and owned the jacket with the specific fabric. This led her to a small group of people.

One night, while staking out one of the suspect's homes, she noticed a figure lurking in the shadows. The figure had a limp and the same build as her attacker. Seizing the moment, Laura confronted the figure. It was a tense standoff, but Laura was prepared. She managed to subdue the figure and called for backup.

When the backup arrived and the figure was apprehended, Laura finally came face to face with her attacker. It was a shocking revelation - the assailant was a member of the local gang, someone who was barely on her radar. But the evidence was undeniable. The shoe print, the fabric, the limp, and now the tattoo - all pointed to him.

However, the identity of the murderer was still a mystery. The assailant was just a pawn in the grand scheme of things, a desperate attempt to derail her investigation. But Laura was not deterred. She knew she was one step closer to uncovering the truth.

5

The Web of Motives

The investigation was now in full swing, with Laura and Mike facing a daunting list of suspects, each potentially linked to the murder of James Thornton. As they delved deeper into the backgrounds of these individuals, the complexity of the case became increasingly apparent.

First on their list were the gang members, the most obvious suspects given the evidence found at the crime scene. The unique shoes and fabric traced back to them, suggesting a motive rooted in Thornton's business conflicts with the gang. However, their solid alibis for the night of the murder posed a significant challenge to the detectives.

Next was Robert Caldwell, Thornton's former business partner, whose presence in Thornton's study hinted at a deeper connection between the two men. Despite having moved away years ago, Caldwell's unresolved business dealings with Thornton cast suspicion on his role in the murder.

The detectives also turned their attention to rival businessmen in town, whose resentment towards Thornton's success may have fueled motives for his demise. Curiously, these businessmen shared similarities with the gang members in their attire, raising questions about their potential involvement.

Meanwhile, the identity of Laura's assailant had been uncovered, but his motive remained elusive. Was he merely a pawn manipulated by more significant forces, or did he harbor personal grievances against Laura or Thornton?

Adding a twist to the investigation was the discovery of Thornton's will, which revealed his decision to leave his entire fortune to charity, bypassing his estranged son. This unexpected revelation thrust the son into the spotlight as a potential suspect, despite his absence from Ravenswood at the time of the murder. Determining his exact whereabouts would be crucial in deciphering his involvement in the crime.

With each suspect presenting a compelling motive and a complex web of connections to unravel, Laura and Mike knew that untangling the truth from the shadows of deception would require meticulous attention to detail and a willingness to confront the darkest secrets lurking within Ravenswood.

6

∿

The Shady Dealings

As Laura and Mike delved deeper into Thornton's business dealings, they uncovered a labyrinth of deceit and treachery that stretched far beyond the confines of the town. Thornton's empire, built on a foundation of ambition and greed, seemed to teeter on the edge of collapse as the detectives peeled back the layers of his carefully constructed facade.

Their investigation led them down a winding path of corporate intrigue and cutthroat competition, where alliances were forged and broken in the pursuit of power. Thornton's rivals lurked in the shadows, their resentment simmering beneath the surface as they vied for control of the town's lucrative industries.

But it wasn't just rival businessmen who had a motive to harm Thornton. The detectives soon discovered that his dealings extended into the realm of politics, where his influence cast a long shadow over the town's governance. Politicians, eager to curry favor with Thornton's wealth and influence, found themselves entangled in a web of corruption and compromise.

As Laura and Mike sifted through the tangled web of connections, they unearthed a trail of breadcrumbs that led them to Thornton's estranged son. Bitter and resentful, the son had long felt overshadowed by his father's success, his grievances simmering beneath the surface like a dormant volcano waiting to erupt.

But perhaps the most intriguing revelation came in the form of an anonymous letter, a cryptic message hinting at a betrayal that could have sealed Thornton's fate. The detectives knew that this could be the breakthrough they had been waiting for, the key to unlocking the secrets hidden within the town's darkest corners.

With each new revelation, Laura and Mike found themselves drawn deeper into the heart of Ravenswood's underworld, where the lines between friend and foe blurred with every passing moment. They knew that the truth was out there, waiting to be uncovered, but they also knew that they were treading on dangerous ground.

The stakes were higher than ever as Laura and Mike raced against time to unravel the mystery before them. With every step they took, they risked uncovering secrets that some would kill to protect. But they were undeterred, their determination unyielding in the face of adversity.

As they pieced together the fragments of evidence, Laura and Mike found themselves on the cusp of a revelation that would shake Ravenswood to its core. The truth, they knew, was a double-edged sword, capable of both healing wounds and reopening old scars.

Yet, for all their progress, the detectives knew that they were still missing a crucial piece of the puzzle. The identity of Thornton's killer remained elusive, a shadowy figure lurking just beyond their reach. But they refused to give up hope, knowing that justice would eventually prevail.

With the town's secrets laid bare before them, Laura and Mike stood on the precipice of discovery, their resolve unshaken by the challenges that lay ahead. For in the heart of Ravenswood, where the echoes of the past lingered like ghosts in the mist, they knew that the truth would ultimately set them free.

7

The Deep Dive

With a myriad of clues and leads spread before them like pieces of a complex puzzle, Laura and Mike knew that their investigation had reached a critical juncture. Each fragment of information, no matter how seemingly insignificant, held the potential to unlock the truth behind the murder mystery haunting Ravenswood.

Revisiting the initial clues that had pointed them towards the local gang, Laura and Mike recognized the importance of thoroughness in their approach. While the shoe print and fabric had initially implicated the gang members, the detectives understood the necessity of exploring all avenues of inquiry. They widened their scope to include local businesses and affluent individuals who shared the same distinctive attire, recognizing that the killer could be hiding in plain sight among the town's elite.

Delving deeper into James Thornton's murky business dealings, Laura and Mike uncovered a labyrinth of intrigue populated by high-profile figures with their own motives for wishing harm upon Thornton. Each individual implicated in the dubious transaction became a potential suspect, adding layers of complexity to an already convoluted case.

The revelation of Thornton's estranged son as a potential beneficiary of the murder raised further questions about familial dynamics and hidden resentments. Despite being abroad at the time of his father's death, the son's exclusion from the will provided a compelling motive that could not be ignored. Yet, confirming or dispelling his involvement hinged upon unraveling the mystery of his whereabouts on the fateful night.

An anonymous tip regarding a clandestine meeting and an astute observation regarding a mysterious limp added new dimensions to the investigation. Laura, recognizing the significance of these leads, resolved to pursue them relentlessly, hopeful that they would provide crucial insights into the tangled web of deception ensnaring Ravenswood.

As they stood at the precipice of discovery, Laura and Mike found themselves confronted with the daunting reality of a case that seemed to grow more intricate with each revelation. Every clue uncovered served only to deepen the enigma surrounding Thornton's murder, leaving the detectives grappling with an ever-expanding web of deceit and uncertainty.

Their investigation took them to the heart of Ravenswood, where the town's secrets lay hidden beneath a veneer of tranquility. Laura and Mike combed through dusty archives and interviewed residents, piecing together a narrative fraught with betrayal and intrigue.

Yet, for every step forward, they encountered obstacles that threatened to derail their progress. Suspects provided alibis, witnesses recanted their statements, and evidence seemed to vanish into thin air. The town itself appeared to conspire against them, its whispers of suspicion mingling with the chill of uncertainty.

Amidst the chaos, Laura and Mike found solace in their partnership, their unwavering commitment to justice fueling their determination to see the case through to its conclusion. They worked tirelessly, their days bleeding into nights as they chased down leads and followed hunches, unwilling to let go of the hope that the truth would eventually reveal itself.

As the investigation progressed, tensions mounted in Ravenswood, the once-quiet streets now simmering with an undercurrent of fear and suspicion. Rumors swirled, fingers pointed, and alliances shifted in the shifting sands of uncertainty.

Laura's near-fatal encounter with her assailant served as a stark reminder of the dangers lurking in the shadows of Ravenswood. Yet, rather than dissuading her, the attack only fueled her determination to uncover the truth. She refused to be intimidated, her resolve strengthened by the knowledge that she was closer than ever to unraveling the mystery.

Meanwhile, Mike delved deeper into the gang's activities, following a trail of breadcrumbs that led him into the heart of the criminal under-world. His efforts unearthed a network of corruption and deceit, reveal-ing the extent of the gang's influence over the town.

With each passing day, Laura and Mike edged closer to the truth, their pursuit of justice unwavering in the face of adversity. They knew that the road ahead would be fraught with peril, but they were undeterred. They were detectives, sworn to uphold the law and protect the innocent, and they would not rest until they had brought James Thornton's killer to justice.

As they prepared to face their greatest challenge yet, Laura and Mike found strength in each other, their partnership a beacon of hope in the darkness that threatened to engulf them. Together, they would confront the shadows of Ravenswood and emerge victorious, their determination unwavering in the face of adversity.

In the end, it would be their resilience and unwavering commitment to justice that would see them through, their faith in each other guiding them through the darkest of nights. For in the heart of Ravenswood, where secrets festered like wounds unhealed, Laura and Mike would shine a light into the shadows and expose the truth that had long been concealed.

As they stood on the brink of revelation, Laura and Mike knew that their journey was far from over. The road ahead would be long and fraught with danger, but they were ready. They were detectives, and they would not rest until justice was served.

8

The Informant's End

The shrill ring of the phone pierces the tranquility of the night, jolting Detectives Laura and Mike from their contemplation of the case's myriad twists and turns. An anonymous caller, his voice quivering with fear, claims to possess vital information regarding Thornton's murder. The promise of a breakthrough crackles in the air, infusing the detectives with a renewed sense of urgency as they hastily prepare to follow the lead.

The journey to the designated meeting place, a desolate warehouse on the outskirts of the city, is fraught with tension. The dim glow of the moon casts elongated shadows across the barren landscape, heightening the sense of unease that permeates the night. Each passing mile brings them closer to the heart of the mystery, yet the anticipation of what awaits them at their destination hangs heavy in the air.

As they approach the warehouse, its imposing silhouette looms ominously against the moonlit sky, a silent sentinel guarding its secrets within. The crunch of gravel beneath their feet echoes in the stillness, a stark contrast to the palpable tension that envelops them. With each step towards the looming structure, the detectives steel themselves for whatever may lie ahead.

Pushing open the creaking door, the detectives are met with a scene straight out of a nightmare. The interior of the warehouse is shrouded in darkness, illuminated only by the feeble beams of their flashlights. Rows of abandoned crates line the walls, their contents obscured by layers of dust and neglect. And there, in the far corner, lies their informant, his lifeless body a chilling testament to the dangers of their pursuit.

The sight of their informant's murder sends a shiver down their spines, a stark reminder of the perilous nature of their investigation. Yet amidst the grim tableau, a glimmer of hope emerges. A set of fresh tire tracks, imprinted in the loose gravel outside the warehouse, offers a potential lead in their quest for answers.

Quickly realizing the significance of the tire tracks, Laura and Mike waste no time in documenting the evidence before them. With meticulous care, they make a cast of the tracks, knowing that it could hold the key to unraveling the mystery surrounding the informant's death. The investigation has taken a dark turn, but the detectives refuse to be deterred.

Back at their office, the detectives pore over the details of the case, their minds buzzing with the possibilities that lie ahead. The murder of their informant has only served to intensify their resolve, fueling their determination to see justice served. The night may be long, but Laura and Mike are prepared to do whatever it takes to bring Thornton's killer to justice.

As the city sleeps, oblivious to the drama unfolding in its shadowy underbelly, Laura and Mike embark on a relentless pursuit of the truth. Every clue, every lead, brings them one step closer to uncovering the dark secrets that lie buried beneath the surface. The hunt is on, and they will not rest until justice is served.

Unmasking Deceit: The Night of Revelations

As Laura and Mike delve deeper into the intricate web of clues and leads, they find themselves drawn into a labyrinth of deception and intrigue. The discovery of the unique shoes and fabric at the high-end boutique sends shockwaves through their investigation, revealing unexpected connections between the city's elite businessmen and members of the local gang. This revelation sparks a flurry of questions about the clandestine alliances and hidden agendas that permeate Ravenswood's shadowy underworld.

Meanwhile, their relentless pursuit of the truth leads them to a breakthrough in the form of the tire tracks. The tracks, traced back to a rare, imported car model, serve as a pivotal clue that links directly to Robert Caldwell, a figure previously overlooked in their investigation. The realization that Caldwell may have a more significant role in Thornton's murder than initially presumed sends ripples of anticipation through the detectives' minds.

As they dig deeper into Caldwell's background, they uncover a tangled web of financial transactions and questionable dealings that cast a sinister shadow over his reputation. With each piece of the puzzle falling into place, Laura and Mike find themselves on the brink of a revelation that could shatter the facade of Ravenswood's tranquility.

Meanwhile, international contacts confirm the alibi of Thornton's estranged son, providing a seemingly solid alibi. However, the sudden influx of unexplained wealth raises suspicions, hinting at a deeper layer of complexity to his involvement in his father's affairs. The detectives are left grappling with the ambiguity of his motives, uncertain of his true role in the unfolding drama.

As the threads of the investigation intertwine, Laura and Mike are faced with a stark realization—the case is far more convoluted than they had ever imagined. The blurred lines between friend and foe, truth and deception, serve as a sobering reminder of the intricate dance of power and intrigue that defines their city.

Yet, with each revelation, the detectives inch closer to unraveling the mystery that has gripped Ravenswood in its vice-like grip. The stage is set for a dramatic showdown, where the masks of the guilty will be stripped away, and the truth will be laid bare for all to see.

Determined to see justice served, Laura and Mike steel themselves for the final confrontation, knowing that the fate of their city hangs in the balance. The game of cat and mouse has reached its climax, and they stand ready to face whatever challenges lie ahead in their quest for truth and redemption.

As the city slumbers in blissful ignorance, Laura and Mike remain vigilant, their resolve unwavering in the face of adversity. For them, the night is not a time of rest but rather a battleground where battles are fought and victories won. The darkness may cloak their actions, but their determination burns bright, illuminating the path to justice amidst the shadows of deceit.

10

The Prodigal Son's Deception

The city's mourning draped like a heavy shroud over its streets, the weight of grief palpable in the air. Among the throngs of mourners at the businessman's funeral, the presence of his estranged son stood out like a solitary figure against the backdrop of collective sorrow. His sudden return to Ravenswood stirred whispers of speculation, casting a shadow of suspicion over his intentions.

The detectives, Laura and Mike, couldn't ignore the son's reappearance, especially considering his recent windfall of wealth. Their investigation into his background unearthed a troubling connection to illegal drug dealings with the local drug lord, adding a sinister layer to the already murky waters of the case. The revelation of this link sent shockwaves through their investigation, raising the stakes even higher.

The discovery of a new will, bequeathing the entirety of the businessman's wealth to his son, sent ripples of unease through the detectives' minds. The timing seemed too convenient, fueling suspicions about the son's motives and his potential involvement in his father's untimely demise. Was he a grieving son seeking his rightful inheritance, or was there a darker truth lurking beneath the surface?

As Laura and Mike delved deeper into the son's tangled web of connections, they found themselves navigating a labyrinth of deceit and betrayal. The intricate dance between the son, the drug lord, and the newfound wealth painted a picture of intrigue and danger, where every revelation only served to deepen the mystery.

But the detectives remained steadfast in their pursuit of the truth, undeterred by the complexity of the case. With each piece of the puzzle they uncovered, they inched closer to unraveling the tangled web of deceit that had ensnared their city. The stakes had never been higher, and the pressure to uncover the truth weighed heavily on their shoulders.

Despite the mounting challenges and the ever-present threat of danger, Laura and Mike refused to waver in their resolve. They knew that they were on the cusp of a breakthrough, that the answers they sought lay just beyond their grasp. The game of cat and mouse had reached its climax, and they were determined to emerge victorious.

As they prepared to confront the son and the drug lord, Laura and Mike braced themselves for the final showdown. The shadows of deceit loomed large over Ravenswood, but they refused to be intimidated. Armed with determination and unwavering resolve, they stepped into the fray, ready to face whatever challenges lay ahead.

The city held its breath as the detectives closed in on their suspects, the tension thickening with each passing moment. Every clue, every lead, brought them one step closer to uncovering the truth, to exposing the secrets that had long been buried beneath the surface.

And then, finally, the moment of reckoning arrived. In a dramatic climax that unfolded against the backdrop of Ravenswood's darkest secrets, Laura and Mike confronted the son and the drug lord, unmasking the truth and bringing the reign of deception to an end.

As the dust settled and the city breathed a collective sigh of relief, Laura and Mike stood victorious, their perseverance and determination shining as beacons of hope in the face of adversity. The story of Ravenswood's murder mystery had reached its conclusion, but for the detectives, the journey was far from over.

11

The Unseen Alibi: Robert
Caldwell's Enigma

The shock of the businessman's murder lingered over the city like a dark cloud, casting a pall of unease over its once bustling streets. But amidst the chaos and uncertainty, a new name surfaced from the depths of the shadows - Robert Caldwell. The discovery of tire tracks at the murder scene seemingly pointed the finger of suspicion squarely at him, sending ripples of speculation through the community. Yet, as the detectives soon discovered, the truth was far more elusive than it first appeared.

Bringing Caldwell in for questioning was just the beginning of a tangled web of contradictions and half-truths. His unexpected revelation about his stolen vehicle added a perplexing layer to the mystery, leaving the detectives grappling with the unsettling possibility of a carefully crafted alibi. Was Caldwell truly an innocent victim of circumstance, or was he a master manipulator adept at obscuring his true intentions?

As the detectives delved deeper into Caldwell's past, they unearthed a labyrinth of secrets and lies. His enigmatic persona seemed to blur the lines between innocence and guilt, leaving them questioning every lead and suspect. The stolen vehicle, while initially seeming like a stroke of luck for Caldwell's defense, only served to deepen their suspicions, adding fuel to the fire of their investigation.

With each twist and turn, the detectives found themselves navigating a landscape fraught with uncertainty. The stolen vehicle created a tantalizing link to the murder, yet it also raised more questions than answers. Was Caldwell a pawn in a larger conspiracy, or was he the cunning puppet master pulling the strings from the shadows?

The game of cat and mouse reached new heights as the detectives raced against time to uncover the truth hidden beneath layers of deception. Every clue, every lead, brought them closer to unraveling the enigma surrounding Caldwell and his elusive alibi. But with each step forward, the shadows seemed to grow darker, obscuring their path and clouding their judgment.

The city held its breath as the detectives played their hand in this high-stakes game of shadows and illusions. With the weight of suspicion bearing down upon them, they knew they had to tread carefully, lest they fall prey to the same deceptions they sought to unravel. The truth was out there, waiting to be discovered, but it would require cunning and perseverance to bring it to light.

As the investigation intensified, the detectives found themselves drawn deeper into Caldwell's world, where nothing was as it seemed. They walked a fine line between truth and deception, their every move scrutinized by unseen forces lurking in the shadows. But they refused to be deterred, their determination unwavering in the face of adversity.

The stage was set for a dramatic showdown, where the lines between ally and adversary blurred with every passing moment. With the city as their backdrop and the truth as their prize, the detectives embarked on a perilous journey to uncover the secrets hidden within Caldwell's tangled web of lies.

As they pursued the elusive truth, the detectives found themselves confronted with a series of challenges that tested their resolve and pushed them to their limits. But they remained steadfast in their quest for justice, their unwavering commitment to uncovering the truth driving them forward against all odds.

With each revelation, the puzzle pieces began to fall into place, painting a clearer picture of Caldwell's involvement in the murder. Yet, even as the evidence mounted against him, the detectives knew that they were still missing a crucial piece of the puzzle, a piece that would ultimately lead them to the truth they sought.

As they closed in on Caldwell, the tension in the air crackled with anticipation, the city holding its breath as the final act of this gripping drama played out. In the end, it would be up to the detectives to unravel the mysteries of Caldwell's enigmatic alibi and expose the truth hidden beneath the surface of their seemingly tranquil town.

12

The Drug Lord's Dilemma: A Trail of Shadows

The city's skyline shimmered like a tapestry of stars, each light telling its own story against the backdrop of the night. But tonight, the rhythm of the city was discordant, disrupted by the reverberations of a murder that had shaken its very foundation. In the midst of this dissonance emerged a figure from the shadows, a man whose name struck fear into the hearts of many - the local drug lord.

Laura and Mike, two of the city's finest detectives, found themselves thrust into the heart of this underworld, tasked with untangling the web of mystery and danger that surrounded the drug lord. Their objective was clear - to uncover the drug lord's connection to the murder of the prominent businessman. But as they soon discovered, the path to truth was far from straightforward.

Their informants, denizens of the city's underbelly, whispered tales of a tumultuous relationship between the drug lord and the businessman. It was a narrative woven with threads of power, control, and a father's desperate bid to save his son from the clutches of crime.

The businessman, a titan of industry with a reputation for ruthlessness, had stumbled upon the drug lord's darkest secret - a lucrative cocaine trafficking operation stretching across Europe. Determined to pull his son from the brink of destruction, the businessman sought to enlist his aid in running his legitimate empire. But in challenging the drug lord, he had unwittingly sealed his own fate.

Despite the palpable tension between the two adversaries, concrete evidence linking the drug lord to the murder remained elusive. The crime scene, meticulously combed over by forensic experts, yielded no trace of the drug lord's presence. Witnesses were scarce, and informants remained tight-lipped, their allegiance to the drug lord outweighing their loyalty to justice.

Laura and Mike found themselves at a crossroads, grappling with the frustrating reality of their investigation. The drug lord loomed large as a suspect, yet without irrefutable proof, they were powerless to bring him to justice. With each twist and turn in the case, the labyrinth of their inquiry grew ever more complex.

But the detectives refused to be deterred by the shadows that threatened to engulf them. Armed with dogged determination and an unwavering commitment to truth, they pressed onward, determined to unravel the enigma that lay at the heart of their city.

As they delved deeper into the case, Laura and Mike began to realize that the city itself was not merely a backdrop to their investigation, but a character in its own right. A city of contrasts, where gleaming skyscrapers stood in stark contrast to dimly lit alleyways, it held secrets both hidden and revealed.

With each move they made, Laura and Mike understood that the stakes were higher than ever before. Every decision had the potential to bring them one step closer to the truth or plunge them further into the depths of the unknown. Yet, undeterred by the daunting task ahead, they forged ahead with steely resolve and unwavering resolve.

13

Unveiling Deception

In the wake of Robert Caldwell's startling disclosure, Detectives Laura and Mike found themselves grappling with a whirlwind of thoughts and emotions. Laura, ever the skeptic, couldn't shake the feeling that there was more to Caldwell's alibi than met the eye. She had a gut instinct, honed over years of experience, that told her there was a deeper truth waiting to be uncovered beneath the surface of Caldwell's carefully crafted facade.

Meanwhile, Mike wrestled with his own doubts and uncertainties, his mind racing as he tried to piece together the fragments of evidence they had gathered so far. The tire tracks, the stolen vehicle, Caldwell's murky past - each clue seemed to paint a picture of a man with something to hide, but what that something was remained tantalizingly out of reach.

As they delved deeper into Caldwell's past, Laura and Mike found themselves confronted with a maze of contradictions and half-truths that seemed designed to confound their efforts. There were gaps in Caldwell's story, inconsistencies that hinted at a darker truth lurking beneath the surface. But without concrete evidence, they were left grasping at shadows, their doubts gnawing at the edges of their resolve.

Yet, even in the face of uncertainty, Laura and Mike refused to give up hope. They knew that the truth was out there, waiting to be discovered, and they were determined to uncover it no matter the cost. With each passing day, their resolve grew stronger, fueled by the knowledge that the fate of Ravenswood hung in the balance.

But time was running out, and the pressure was mounting. With suspicion mounting and the weight of expectation bearing down upon them, Laura and Mike knew that they could ill afford to falter. Every moment lost was a step closer to oblivion, a descent into the abyss of uncertainty where truth and falsehood intertwined in a bewildering dance.

In the heart of Ravenswood, where secrets festered like festering wounds, Laura and Mike stood on the brink of discovery. But the shadows of deception loomed large, threatening to engulf them in their depths. Only by acting swiftly and decisively could they hope to expose the truth hidden beneath the surface, lest they succumb to the darkness that lurked within.

As they combed through the city's shadows, piecing together the fragments of evidence that might hold the key to unlocking Caldwell's secrets, Laura and Mike knew that their journey was far from over. With danger lurking around every corner and betrayal lurking in the shadows, they braced themselves for the final showdown, where the fate of Ravenswood would be decided once and for all.

14

∾

Veil of Obscurity

Laura and Mike find themselves immersed in the heart of the city's underworld, where the drug lord's influence reigns supreme. As they navigate through the murky alleys and clandestine meeting spots, they are acutely aware of the ever-present danger lurking in the shadows, threatening to engulf them at every turn.

With each step they take, the line between right and wrong blurs, and the distinction between ally and adversary becomes increasingly difficult to discern. They tread cautiously, mindful of the treacherous web of deceit that surrounds them, knowing that one wrong move could spell disaster.

Despite the pervasive sense of uncertainty, Laura and Mike are fueled by a newfound determination to expose the truth hidden beneath the layers of secrecy. Their encounter with a mysterious informant provides them with a glimmer of hope, offering tantalizing clues that promise to unravel the intricate web of corruption woven by the drug lord and his cohorts.

As they delve deeper into the heart of darkness, Laura and Mike confront their own fears and doubts, grappling with the moral complexities of their mission. The allure of justice beckons them forward, driving them to persevere in the face of mounting danger and insurmountable odds.

Yet, for all their resolve, they cannot shake the gnawing sense of foreboding that hangs over them like a dark cloud. The drug lord's reach extends far beyond the confines of the city, casting a long shadow that threatens to eclipse their efforts and plunge them into the abyss of despair.

With each passing moment, the pressure mounts, and the stakes soar ever higher. Laura and Mike find themselves locked in a deadly game of cat and mouse, racing against time to uncover the truth before it's too late. Every decision they make, every lead they follow, brings them closer to the brink of disaster.

But amidst the chaos and uncertainty, a flicker of hope remains. Laura and Mike cling to the belief that justice will prevail, that the light of truth will ultimately pierce through the veil of obscurity and illuminate the path forward. With unwavering determination, they press on, determined to see their mission through to its end, no matter the cost.

As they inch closer to their goal, they realize that their journey is far from over. The road ahead is fraught with peril, and the challenges they face are formidable. Yet, they refuse to back down, driven by a shared commitment to see justice served and the forces of darkness vanquished once and for all.

In the end, it will be their courage, their resilience, and their unwavering faith in the power of truth that will see them through. For in the darkest of nights, when all hope seems lost, it is often in the depths of despair that the light shines brightest, guiding the way to redemption and salvation.

15

The Illusion of Guilt

The city's whispers grew louder as Laura and Mike delved deeper into their investigation, each clue leading them closer to the heart of darkness. With the weight of suspicion bearing down upon them, they found themselves at a crossroads, faced with a revelation that threatened to upend everything they thought they knew.

As they sifted through the evidence, a pattern began to emerge - a pattern that pointed squarely to the local drug lord. The fingerprints at the crime scene, the eyewitness accounts, even the faintest whispers of informants - all seemed to converge on one man, casting a shadow of guilt that stretched far and wide.

But Laura and Mike knew better than to trust in appearances alone. As seasoned detectives, they understood that things were not always as they seemed, and that the truth often lurked in the most unexpected of places. And so, with a steely resolve, they set out to uncover the illusion of guilt that threatened to cloud their judgment.

Their investigation led them down a labyrinth of deception, where every turn revealed another layer of the drug lord's carefully constructed facade. Yet amidst the chaos, a glimmer of doubt emerged, a nagging suspicion that all was not as it appeared.

With each passing moment, Laura and Mike grew more convinced that they were being led astray, that the clues they had painstakingly assembled were nothing more than smoke and mirrors. And as they peeled back the layers of deception, they uncovered a truth more sinister than they could have ever imagined.

For lurking in the shadows was a puppet master pulling the strings, orchestrating a grand illusion designed to deflect suspicion and protect his own interests. And as Laura and Mike stared into the abyss, they knew that their greatest challenge lay not in apprehending a criminal, but in exposing the truth hidden beneath the veil of lies.

With newfound determination, they pressed on, their resolve unshakeable in the face of adversity. For they knew that in the heart of Ravenswood, where the echoes of the past lingered like ghosts in the mist, the only way to dispel the darkness was to shine a light on the truth, no matter how elusive it may be.

16

Closing In

The air crackled with tension as Laura and Mike reviewed the evidence meticulously laid out before them. Every shred of information, every painstakingly gathered clue, pointed with unnerving precision to one man: the elusive drug lord whose shadow loomed large over Ravenswood.

Their desks were cluttered with files, photographs, and witness statements, each piece of the puzzle fitting snugly into place. Fingerprints lifted from the crime scene matched those of known associates of the drug lord. Eyewitness accounts placed his henchmen in the vicinity at the time of the murder. And whispers from informants painted a chilling portrait of his iron-fisted rule.

Laura's gaze flickered to Mike, a silent acknowledgment passing between them. They were on the brink of something monumental, a breakthrough that would send shockwaves through the criminal underworld. It was time to bring the drug lord to justice, to strip away the veil of impunity that had shielded him for far too long.

With steely resolve, Laura picked up the phone and dialed the precinct. It was time to set their plan in motion, to mobilize the forces of law and order in a coordinated strike against their elusive quarry. A warrant for a house search was prepared, a legal instrument to pierce the fortress of the drug lord's lair and lay bare his secrets.

As they waited for the cavalry to assemble, Laura and Mike exchanged a wordless exchange, their hearts pounding in anticipation. They knew the risks they faced, the dangers that lurked in the shadows. But they were undeterred, their determination burning bright like a beacon in the night.

Minutes stretched into eternity as they braced themselves for the inevitable confrontation. Finally, the call came - the warrant was signed, the green light given. It was time to move.

With a sense of purpose, Laura and Mike led the charge, a phalanx of officers at their backs. The streets of Ravenswood buzzed with activity as they descended upon the drug lord's stronghold, a fortress of concrete and steel that seemed to mock their efforts.

But Laura and Mike were undaunted, their resolve unshakeable in the face of adversity. With a swift kick, they breached the door, the hinges groaning in protest as they stormed into the belly of the beast.

What they found inside took their breath away - stacks of cash piled high like mountains, drugs stashed away in hidden compartments, weapons of death concealed in plain sight. It was a scene straight out of a nightmare, a testament to the depths of human depravity.

And at the center of it all stood the drug lord, his hands raised in surrender, a look of defeat etched upon his face. The game was up, the illusion shattered. Justice had finally caught up with him, its hand cold and unyielding.

As they led him away in handcuffs, Laura and Mike couldn't help but feel a sense of satisfaction wash over them. They had done it - they had brought a kingpin to his knees, dismantling his empire piece by piece. And as they stepped out into the light of day, they knew that Ravenswood would sleep a little sounder tonight, its streets a little safer thanks to their tireless efforts.

17

A New Dawn

The dawn broke over Ravenswood, casting its golden rays upon a city reborn from the ashes of its darkest hour. The streets, once shrouded in fear and uncertainty, now hummed with the vibrancy of newfound hope. For Laura and Mike, it was a moment of reflection, a chance to look back on the journey that had led them here.

In the aftermath of the drug lord's downfall, the city had undergone a remarkable transformation. With their leader behind bars, his criminal empire lay in ruins, its influence waning with each passing day. The people of Ravenswood emerged from the shadows, their spirits lifted by the promise of a brighter tomorrow.

For Laura and Mike, it was a bittersweet victory, tinged with the memories of those they had lost along the way. James Thornton, the murdered businessman whose death had sparked the chain of events that led them here, was never far from their thoughts. His legacy lived on in the hearts of those who had known him, a reminder of the cost of justice.

But amidst the sorrow, there was also joy - joy in knowing that their efforts had not been in vain, that justice had prevailed in the end. As they walked the streets of Ravenswood, they were greeted with smiles and nods of gratitude, the silent acknowledgment of a city grateful for their service.

As they reached the precinct, a sense of closure washed over them. The case was closed, the loose ends tied, the chapter finally brought to a close. But for Laura and Mike, it was not the end, but rather a new beginning.

For in the heart of Ravenswood, where shadows once lurked and secrets festered, a light now shone bright. It was a light fueled by the courage and determination of two detectives who refused to give up, who fought tirelessly for the truth even when the odds were stacked against them.

And as they looked out over the city they had sworn to protect, they knew that no matter what challenges lay ahead, they would face them together. For in the end, it was not the darkness that defined them, but the light that they carried within - a light that would guide them through even the darkest of nights.

And so, as the sun rose high in the sky, casting its warm embrace upon the city below, Laura and Mike set forth into a new day, their hearts filled with hope and their heads held high. For in the end, they were not just detectives, but guardians of the truth, protectors of the innocent, and champions of justice in a world that sorely needed it.